The Gabby Cats Save the Day

ORCHARD BOOKS

First published in Great Britain in 2023 by Hodder & Stoughton

DreamWorks Gabby's Dollhouse © 2023 DreamWorks Animation LLC. All Rights Reserved

A CIP catalogue record for this book is available from the British Library

ISBN 978 1 40837 186 2

1 3 5 7 9 10 8 6 4 2

Printed and bound in Great Britain by Bell & Bain Ltd, Glasgow

Orchard Books
An imprint of Hachette Children's Group
part of Hodder & Stoughton Limited
Carmelite House
50 Victoria Embankment
London EC4Y 0DZ
An Hachette UK Company
www.hachette.co.uk
www.hachettechildrens.co.uk

The Gabby Cats
Save the Day

Grab your magical cat ears and join
Gabby and the Gabby Cats for
an adventure in the dollhouse!

"Hi! I'm Gabby, and this is Pandy Paws!" Gabby said. "Welcome to my bedroom! Isn't it a-meow-zing?"

Gabby smiled at her real-life cat, who was curled in his cat bed. "And this is Floyd."

"The most cat-tastic thing in my bedroom is . . .
My dollhouse! All my Gabby Cats live in here."

meow, meow, meow!

"Did you hear that sound?" Gabby asked. "That means it's time for the Dollhouse Delivery! Let's see what the surprise is today!"

Gabby pulled a package from her Meow Meow Mailbox. Inside was a little kitty spaceship!

"Kitty Fairy would love this!" she said. "Let's go into the dollhouse and show her!"

Gabby put on her kitty ears. Then she sang a special song and held tight to Pandy's hand!

A few seconds and many sparkles later, Gabby and Pandy Paws were tiny, just like the Gabby Cats!

They landed in the dollhouse in the Fairy Tail Garden.

"I'm over here," Gabby called. "Come on in!"

"Welcome to the dollhouse!" Gabby said. "First things first. Let's find Pandy. Do you see him?"

Suddenly, Pandy jumped out from his hiding spot. "Hug attack!" he cried.

Outside the dollhouse, Pandy is a cuddly toy, but inside, he comes alive!

PANDY PAWS

This sweet kitty loves to eat and is always up for an adventure with Gabby.

Likes to say: Hug attack!

Hobbies: Snuggling – he loves Gabby with all his heart!

Favourite dance Move: Pandy Paw Bump

Fun fact: Pandy can fit many useful items in his trusty bag. He loves filling it with tasty snacks!

You can find Pandy wherever Gabby is.

"I thought I heard you two," said Kitty Fairy. Gabby showed her the spaceship.

"It's cat-tastic!" Kitty Fairy exclaimed.

Just then, CatRat popped up from a secret tunnel!

"Hey! What's all the racket up here?!" he asked.

Kitty Fairy

This tiny cat with fairy wings is gentle and nurturing, and she loves taking care of her friends in the dollhouse.

Likes to say: Flower-rific!

Hobbies: Garden Magic

Fun fact: Kitty Fairy likes to have tea parties in Rainbow Falls.

You can find Kitty Fairy in the Fairy Tail Garden.

CatRat climbed inside the spaceship. "This is the shiniest cat bed I've ever seen!" he said. "Time for my cat nap!" With that, he fell fast asleep . . . and rolled on to the take-off button!

"Oh no! How are we going to get him down?" Pandy asked.

The floating spaceship reminded Gabby of MerCat's bubbles.

"Maybe MerCat has an idea," she said. "To the bathroom!"

CatRat

CatRat is a sneaky cat who loves to play tricks, but at the end of the day, he has a good heart.

Likes to say: Shiny is miney!

Hobbies: Mischief

Fun fact: He reads comic books.

You can find CatRat in the secret passageways of the dollhouse.

Gabby told MerCat all about the spaceship.

"Shimmering sea scales!" MerCat said. "I'm not sure my bubbles can help, but maybe Pillow Cat can find a way. She likes to nap as much as CatRat."

"Good idea, MerCat!" Gabby said. "Let's go find Pillow Cat. To the bedroom!"

"Thanks, MerCat!" Pandy said.

 # MerCat

MerCat is part cat, part mermaid. She uses spa science to mix bath bombs, lotions and potions, and she has a spa science solution for almost every problem.

Likes to say: Shimmering sea scales!

Hobbies: Spa science

Fun fact: MerCat has the best spa parties.

You can find MerCat in the bathroom.

In the bedroom, Gabby told Pillow Cat about the spaceship.

"When I need to think of a new idea, I rest my eyes and let my imagination take over," Pillow Cat said.

"Let's give it a try!" Gabby cheered.

Gabby closed her eyes and dreamed up an idea.

When she opened her eyes, she said, "Thanks, Pillow Cat. I know who can help! To the kitchen!"

Pillow Cat

Pillow Cat loves to dream up stories and act them out with the Gabby cats.

Likes to say: Let's roll with it!

Hobbies: Napping and dreaming

Fun fact: Pillow Cat has a magical dress-up closet with costumes for everyone!

You can find Pillow Cat in the bedroom.

"Oh, sprinkles!" Cakey Cat cried when he heard about CatRat. "I don't know how to help! But baking always makes me feel better. Want to bake some sticky cat paws?"

They baked the treats, and Pandy put one in his pouch. Suddenly, the spaceship floated past the kitchen window.

"Oh no!" Gabby said. "Pandy, let's see if Baby Box can help. To the craft room!"

 ## Cakey Cat

Cakey is clever yet sensitive, and sometimes he cries sprinkles when things go wrong, or cries sprinkles of joy when things go right!

Likes to say: Sprinkle party!

Hobbies: Cooking, baking and making smoothies

Fun fact: Cakey has a cupcake cousin named Pattycake.

You can find Cakey in the kitchen.

In the craft room, Gabby and Pandy asked Baby Box for help.

"I have a crafty-rific idea!" Baby Box said.

They worked to make a long chain to catch the spaceship.

"Now we know how to save CatRat, but we need to wake him up first . . ."
Baby Box said.

"I have an a-meow-zing idea! Pandy, to the music room!" Gabby said.

BaBy BOX

This cardboard cutie is inventive, hardworking and creative. When there's a problem, Baby Box is always eager to find a crafty solution.

Likes to say: Crafty-rific!

Hobbies: Crafting, decorating and building

Fun fact: Baby Box likes to climb and swing on a pom-pom rope.

You can find Baby Box in the craft room.

Gabby and Pandy found DJ Catnip at his turntables making music.

"DJ Catnip, we are hoping you can wake up CatRat," Gabby said.

"On it!" DJ Catnip said. "Let's turn the music up loud. It's the only thing to do!"

DJ CatNip

From jamming on instruments to mixing up beats, DJ Catnip uses music to bring the Gabby Cats together, help them find their groove and remind them anything is possible.

Likes to say: Boogie on over here!

Hobbies: Playing his tuba

Fun fact: His music room has a xylosofa you can play with your bottom.

You can find DJ Catnip in the music room.

It was time to zoom to the Fairy Tail Garden. In the playroom, Carlita sped over to meet them.

"Kitty Fairy told me CatRat is out of the dollhouse!" she said. "Do you want a ride?"

Gabby and Pandy hopped in. "Thanks, Carlita! Let's go save CatRat!"

CARLITA

Carlita is part race car, part cat. She loves to drive all around the dollhouse helping her friends, especially when it means racing up the ramp to the Fairy Tail Garden.

Likes to say: Beep beep! Hop in!

Hobbies: Playing games

Fun fact: She loves pretending to be a taxi, train, fire engine and aeroplane.

You can find Carlita in the playroom.

Outside the dollhouse, CatRat was finally awake. "Get me out of here!" he shouted. Floyd thought the spaceship was a cat toy!

Gabby threw the chains they'd made to catch the spaceship, but they bounced off.

Then Gabby remembered the sticky cat paws they made with Cakey Cat.

"Pandy! Any extra sticky paws in your pouch?" she asked. Pandy pulled out a sticky paw, and Gabby stuck one to the end of the chain and threw it at the spaceship. It stuck!

Together, everyone pulled CatRat back.

"CatRat, you're safe!" his friends said.

All the Gabby Cats hugged him. Everyone was happy he was back!

Gabby turned to her friends and smiled. "Now let's take this spaceship out for a proper spin!"